BIKER'S PUNISHED LITTLE

ABDL MM Romance

Jerry Hastings

ISBN: 9798817920987
Imprint: Independently published

1st edition

Cover design by: Jerry Hastings

CONTENTS

CHAPTER 1

Caleb

I stepped out of the building and my feet screeched to a halt when I found the most amazing thing in the world. It was just idling there, almost like it was waiting for me.

The most amazing, eye-catching bike in the world. I was a little surprised that I didn't notice it until now, to be honest. I should have already noticed it before.

It was mostly black with details made of chrome and silver. The light was turned off, as it should be. I couldn't spot the owner of the bike anywhere nearby, I noticed after turning my head left and right. A little breath came out of my mouth, showing my relief.

One of the reasons behind that was that the bike was very different from a common, mundane one. That one was so different that I knew it belonged to one of those... *bikers*. Just thinking about them was enough to make my heart speed up, and not in a good way, too.

They were dangerous, and overly so. When they had their eyes set on something, they never held back when trying to achieve it.

Even though it was a little dangerous to approach the bike, I was still going to do it. I smiled, even though the smile was small and insignificant. I weighed each of my footsteps, crossing the path between the cars and other motorcycles.

Even though they were here in this parking space, they didn't catch my attention the same way that particular motorcycle did, which was one of the reasons why I was so interested in it.

I took another step closer to the motorcycle, stopping when I thought I heard voices coming this way. But I was only hearing things, I could tell. I could also hear the cars and other motorcycles driving on the roads around me, but I had already tuned them out.

I was close enough now that I could make out all the details of the bike, and even though I knew that it was a mistake, I put my hand on it and started to move it around the parts of it, feeling just how perfect it was.

It was slightly hot, too, and it wasn't because of the sunlight. I knew we were in the middle of the summer season, but the motorcycle was mostly in the shade, and the air around it wasn't that hot.

I guessed that meant the motorcycle was in use until not too long ago. Whoever owned it had to be nearby. Thinking that, my heart sped up even more than it already was.

I didn't want to encounter the biker that owned it, even though I also didn't want to move away from the bike right now.

I pulled out my phone, snapping photos of the motorcycle. Maybe I was making a mistake, but it wasn't like the owner of the motorcycle was going to care about this, or that he even used the Internet, for that matter.

I knew what they were like. Bikers from the local club – The Roarers – weren't like that. They were old school, and always prone to breaking the law whenever it suited them. And yet, it was for that reason I just didn't want to come across them. I knew very well the implications of that, which was something that frightened me.

And I was just snapping another photo when I heard footsteps stopping behind me. For a moment, I froze up. But then I realized that I had to do something.

If I didn't, whoever was behind me and who certainly had his eyes on me would be pretty pissed.

It was for that reason I slowly turned around as the man that was behind me said, "Looks like someone likes my bike."

It was an innocent phrase, but it still caught me off guard. I didn't expect it. When he said it, it was almost like I was doing something wrong and he just caught me red-handed. I felt my cheeks flushing, and it wasn't the first time that this was happening.

My eyes sized up the man that was in front of me. He was much taller than me, a couple of years older, his hair was blond, and he had a beard on his face. It was a little rough, showing me that he hadn't shaved in a while. And yet, he was still quite handsome.

He was making me feel something that was a little more than a crush I had on him. I wasn't going to say that it was love or anything of the sort, but I could feel my prick jumping in my pants, which was something that didn't happen often.

I could already imagine him as my caregiver, even though there was no chance that he could ever become that. He was a biker and his leather jacket told me so. He was probably straight, even though, looking down, I couldn't see a ring on his marriage finger.

It could be that he was single, but as long as he looked straight, then he probably was. Not to mention that most bikers probably didn't let gay men into their clubs as well. They were usually quite conservative, I reminded myself.

Rubbing the back of my head, I replied, "It's a pretty cool bike, actually. You should be proud of it."

"I am," he said and then he didn't say anything else, which was quite unnerving. I could feel my skin prickling, which was something that didn't happen often. Even though I could be nervous sometimes, I usually never felt this much anxiety.

A moment later, when I thought I was going to pass out, he climbed up on the bike. He rolled the handlebars, making the bike roar to life. The sound that came from the engine was nothing short of impressive, and so much more than that, too.

I was legitimately frightened of it.

"Do you like the sound of it as well?" He asked after he stopped rolling the handlebars. Even though I liked the way he was doing that, I was relieved that he stopped.

"Yes, I do," I answered, my eyes raking him. There was something about him, and even though he was wearing his leather jacket and jeans pants, I could tell that he worked out often.

His muscles were straining against his clothes, and I could also see a little hint of his chest hair peeking out through his shirt.

I couldn't help but imagine myself putting my head on his chest, letting time pass without either of us doing anything. I could also imagine myself sleeping like that, which was suddenly making my prick jump in my pants once again.

But then I reminded myself that even if he was into men, there was no way that he was also into ABDL. I wasn't a hard-core enjoyer of the lifestyle, but it resonated with me. It made me feel something special, something I thought I didn't have.

"This is Memory, and I paid a pretty penny for it. You can take as many pictures of it as you want."

And when he said that, I was even more surprised. I thought he was going to be pissed off at me for snapping photos of his motorcycle without permission.

After all, it was like his little treasure, something he loved more than pretty much everything else in his life. I knew what things were like when it came to bikers, and that was pretty much spot on.

I felt I was almost stumbling with my words. "Uhh, thanks, but I've already gotten enough of them."

"Really? That's a pity." And when he turned the front of the bike to the right, my ears picked up a roaring, frightening sound in the distance. It then took no more than a couple of seconds for other motorcycles to show up in the parking space by the administrative building on campus.

I could see the patches on their chests and it showed me that they were from the local bike club as well. I was surprised that the biker I just met, who I promised to myself I wasn't going to stumble across, was nicer than I thought, but they were still who they were.

Lawbreakers, criminals, and even much worse than that. After all, the one percent patch on their chests told me as much.

"My name is Rhys. What's yours?" He asked, holding out his hand. I knew it shouldn't take it, but I still felt compelled to. Maybe it was something about the way he was looking at me with his piercing eyes that was doing it, but the truth was that I still shook his hand. Just like everything else about the man himself, it was massive, powerful, and was showing off his confidence. When it came down to it, he was always like that, I imagined. Always overconfident, always thinking only about himself, which was another reason why I could never fall in love with him.

And even though I knew I was making yet another mistake, I said, "I'm Caleb, and it's nice to meet you."

CHAPTER 2

Rhys

Some people would call it 'love at first sight,' but I called it something different. It was nothing more than a crush, and I was thinking of him as something akin to a treasure.

Like the bike that I bought, Memory. Something that I could use, could have with me, put in my house, and almost... consume. Though, thinking of it that way was a little weird. It was for that reason that I brushed it aside, too.

I stepped into the club, but this club wasn't my motorcycle club. It was a different club, meant for someone like me that wasn't interested in love. The environment was quite heavy, the atmosphere was thick, and I could even see the smoke or the mist of something in the air, floating just above the ground.

The smell from inside it was different from what most people would think. It smelled of strawberry and also of something else I couldn't put my finger on.

It was artificially sprayed inside the room, and it was actually quite good. It made the atmosphere inside the club much more enticing and welcoming.

I stopped in front of the desk and the guy that was behind me asked, "So, which wristband do you want this time, Rhys?" He winked, but I wasn't interested. All I wanted to do here was to pass the time, which I was going to do. Tomorrow morning, we had a little assignment that we had to do for the president of our MC, and I couldn't wait for it.

It was going to be a little rough, even dangerous, but equally exciting. We weren't going to do anything outside of the law, though.

The clerk behind the desk held out different wristbands for it, and I chose the green one. It was bright green and it felt snug on my forearm after it was put around it. I turned my arm to check it out more carefully, and I was happy with it.

The green wristband told everyone in the club that I was willing to do something different tonight, that it was a little kinkier than normal.

I was a caregiver or, in other words, a Daddy, though I didn't like to use the word much. I knew that it was pretty much the most famous in the world of little ones, but I couldn't care less about that.

Being someone's Daddy meant that I was a little more than their romantic partner. And even being their 'romantic partner' was enough to put me off, too. I just didn't believe in love – or not anymore, anyway.

I believed in something else, and that I was born to take whatever I wanted from whoever stood in my way. It was for that reason that I was always called a jerk, and even though it was supposed to make me rethink that part of me, it always did the opposite.

And I just didn't want any of that, not right now anyway.

"You are good to go, Rhys," the attendant said after winking again, and even though it was jarring, I welcomed it. I stepped further inside the club, finding myself in the main room. It was packed with members, first-timers, and other kinds of people. Most of them were forgettable. I didn't come here looking for love, but for something else.

I wanted someone that was also in the world of roleplaying as 'little and caregiver,' and I wondered if this time it was going to be easy to find a candidate. Sometimes, it was difficult. ABDL and age play weren't exactly famous in this kind of scene – at least, not in Hope River.

And talking about Hope River, it was a small town in the middle of nowhere. And when I said 'in the middle of nowhere' I meant that it was so isolated that we couldn't even go to a big city nearby to do things that we couldn't here. Nevertheless, it was growing, especially thanks to the shopping malls that were being built around here.

I already went to one of them, and it was better than I thought. Still not as good as the shopping malls I visited in New York City, which was the biggest city close to this one.

I sighed, finding myself in the middle of the room and scanning it. I was hoping I was going to find at least one person that was also wearing the same kind of wristband, and I couldn't.

I checked pretty much every person that was in the same room, but I was disappointed when I found out that there was nobody.

I could hear the pounding music in my ears, and it was everywhere. It was drowning my thoughts, which was excellent. The assignment that I was going to have tomorrow morning with the president was something I was looking forward to, but there was also a big problem with it, and that was the fact that it was detail-oriented. I needed to pay attention to everything that was going to unravel at the place where we were going to hit, and that thought alone was already stressing me out.

I sat on a couch, putting my hands on my lap. I closed my eyes and tried to tune out everything that was happening around me, but that was more difficult than I thought.

And when I reopened my eyes, I found someone sitting by my side. My eyes widened when I realized that he was none other than Caleb, the little guy I met on the college's campus.

Even though the environment in the club was dark, he still looked as young as he did then, and while I knew that nothing would ever happen between us, I was excited about something else.

I just checked his arm and noticed that he had the same wristband I had! It was bright green, shining in the darkness of the room. I could tell that he was a little nervous, thanks to the way that he kept on wringing his hands.

And yet, the fact that he decided to sit by my side meant something important. Something that was already making my cock stir in my pants.

I noticed the volume under his pants, something that most people would have overlooked. But as someone that was a caregiver and liked to play with diapers, my eyes noticed it immediately. It was so exciting that it was making my heart speed up, which was something that didn't happen often with me.

"You're Caleb, aren't you?" I asked, glancing down at his wristband one more time to make sure that I wasn't imagining things. And I really wasn't. He had the wristband on his arm, and given that I was the only other one on the premises with it, I knew that he possibly wanted to role-play with me.

"Yeah, that's me. We met on campus earlier today."

"Well, in case you've forgotten my name, it's Rhys," I said, and then I added, "and it looks like you're looking for the same thing I'm looking for. I never thought you were a little."

He rubbed the back of his head, showing even more of his nervousness. "I'm like that. I'm always different from everyone I meet, including you. I take it that you aren't a little as well?"

I shook my head. "I'm not. I'm a caregiver."

"So, you are a Daddy."

"I don't like that term, actually."

His eyes widened, and he shifted away from me slightly. The movement was very gentle, but my trained eyes still perceived it. I knew he wasn't going to take that well, but I wasn't going to do anything about it. Since we were going to do this, I needed to be upfront about the things I thought.

"Why not?" He asked. I knew that Caleb was curious about it, but I didn't want to be talking about it right now.

And he must've noticed that, for he waved his hand in the air. "It's okay. You don't have to tell me anything if you don't want to."

And in the meantime, I was trying to convince myself that I wasn't a creep. He was much younger than me, probably by more than a decade. Anyone that didn't know us would accuse me of trying to take advantage of him, and especially the old people that lived in this town would say that. It was one reason why I was a little wary of taking this a step further. Even though the club was located almost outside the town, word would still get around. People would find out about it, including the members of The Roarers, and I didn't even want to think about what would happen if that came to pass.

And yet, I felt inclined to do it with him.

CHAPTER 3

Caleb

I didn't think I was going to come across him, much less that he was gay, and even less that he was ABDL. My head was spinning, and I was having difficulty coming up with the right words to say. He was seated on the couch, by my side, and was already looking the other way.

I didn't know if it was something I said, but I was getting worried about it nonetheless.

"It's pretty obvious that nothing is going to happen between us," he lamented, standing up and when he was already making his way toward the exit door, I latched my hand around his hand. He stopped, but didn't look over his shoulder and at me.

He was just standing there, and my head tuned out everything that was happening around me. Around us, to be more precise. My mind was focused only on us. There was something about Rhys that kept on pulling me to him, and it was intoxicating.

It was addictive. I had never felt something so strong before for someone that wasn't my mother. Growing up, she was the only one that cared about me. My father hated me, as was usually the case for young, gay guys like myself that were also little ones.

I came out to him that I was gay, but withheld the last part. He didn't need to know anything about it, and even though he was still alive, I didn't plan on telling him anything about it.

"You should let go of my hand," he growled, and even though

his voice was quite frightening, I didn't do what he wanted. As far as I knew, he was in the club, was also wearing the same kind of wristband, and that meant he was looking for someone like me.

I'd scoured the city and never found anyone that was also like me, even though I had some suspicions. I had to take advantage of this opportunity.

It was for that reason, among others, that I was reluctant to let go of him. I wanted to do this one special thing with Rhys, and I was pretty sure he was thinking the same thing, even though he didn't want to tell me anything about it.

He wasn't going to say that he was wrong about it. When it came down to it, Rhys was like pretty much everyone else. He was always too proud of himself and had a big ego.

"I'm going to, but how about we go upstairs, pick a room, and then we can find out more about each other? Or maybe we shouldn't even do that and we could, instead, have a little fun."

That was my proposal, and I was hoping he was going to accept it. My heart was even speeding up even more than it already was. There was a very good chance that he was going to accept it.

He sighed and it wasn't because he wasn't enjoying this, but because he wasn't completely okay with this side of him. And yet, when our eyes met, I knew he was already changing his mind about it. I didn't want to say it, not to his face, but there was no denying I was his type. It wasn't that he was looking for younger men like me, but that it was just that. I was his type. I was a little shorter than him, a little scrawny but not too much so, and my skin was still devoid of imperfections.

"If we are going to do this, I need to know that I have your okay," Rhys demanded, moving his hand so that it was gripping mine, and even though it wasn't a strong grip, I knew that he meant it.

He knew about the implications that came with dating someone over 10 years younger than him, and he was wary of that. I could certainly see where he was coming from, but it wasn't going to stop me, or him.

"You have my okay. I'm young, but I'm not stupid. I know that you are like 10 years older than me, and it's really okay."

"It's more than that. I just don't want people to think that I'm taking advantage of you."

"That's bullshit. I'm an adult now, and you should treat me as such."

His hand was so heavy and calloused that it was stirring something different in me, and I couldn't help but wonder what I would feel like when I was roleplaying with him. I even had a dirty little plan I was going to set in motion, and my heart was excited about it.

I never had this opportunity before, thinking about all the times I came to this club, hoping that I was going to find a Daddy Dom, only to come out of it empty-handed.

"Whatever." And that was more him, I thought with a smile on my face. I loved it when he was so direct and ruthless with his words. It was really something that didn't happen often with the people that lived here in Hope River.

"So, are we doing this or not?" I asked, tugging his arm. I was going to take him upstairs and then into one of the available rooms. After the initial bump and resistance, he was already much more willing. Rhys was coming along with me, and I didn't have to force him to do anything.

In no moment at all, he let go of my hand and then opened the door with a key he had. The interior of the room was just as I thought it was. Inviting, but also a little frightening. It was different from the main room of the club, and that was curious.

He closed the door behind me, and I could tell that this room wasn't used here often. It was made specifically for ABDL dynamics, and given that the club didn't receive enough littles and Daddies here, it meant that it was never used as often as it should be, which was a pity.

Now that we were here, we were going to do something about that, I thought amusingly. I just couldn't hide the smile on my face.

"It's hot in here," he said, taking off his shirt. I didn't expect him to do that, which came as a surprise to me. I was overwhelmed by what my eyes were seeing, and I didn't know how to cope with it.

All I knew was that his body was godly, perfect, and I wanted to be sliding my hand over his curves for what felt like hours. If it was possible to do that, especially tonight, I would feel like my day was fulfilling.

I thought he was going to turn around and chuckle at my reaction, but he didn't. I supposed he was still a little conflicted about 'dating' someone so much younger, but he wasn't saying anything else about it.

The room was different. It was equipped with pretty much everything we were going to need, or could even need. And without saying anything else, I was already going on all fours on the floor.

Then, I started to crawl around and pretend that I was a little boy. It was so exciting that my heart was speeding up again. I knew that it was going to be happening quite often with me from now on.

He chuckled, finally showing something different from his usual, cold self. I knew that Rhys was very different from the biker persona that always exuded out of him, but I never thought that he was going to show me he could find something funny. Regardless, I was just rambling and it didn't matter.

It was for that reason that he even picked me up, letting me wrap my legs around his body. I could feel his muscles against my legs, and it was turning me on so much I was already hard. But this, what we were doing, was far from the peak of what I wanted to do with him.

And noticing that, he reached out with his hand and picked up the pacifier that was on a small table. I knew that it wasn't used, but even if it was, I wouldn't be too opposed to putting it into my mouth. The reason behind that was that everything was happening too fast in my mind.

I was overexcited, and that was something that never happened often with me. My life was always so boring, which was one of the reasons why I was enjoying this so much.

"Looks like someone is already a little too excited for his own good," he said, settling me on the floor. He let me crawl around him, which I did while showing no shame.

I knew that tonight was going to be special, and it was going to leave a lasting mark on it.

CHAPTER 4

I knew he was going to be over excited about it, and I already brushed aside the fact that he was much younger than me. He was here, he was an adult, and he was also willing to keep doing this with me.

The room where we were was a little dark to set the right mood, and that coupled with the moody lighting and the aroma in the air made me feel like being someone different from my usual self.

Even though I didn't want to admit it, what my eyes were seeing, the cute little man on the floor and that was crawling around... He was already making me impossibly hard. I just couldn't hide my boner in my pants any longer, and it was showing.

It was for that reason that Caleb winked at me, his eyes glancing down and finding my crotch. I had already seen that face so many times I knew what it meant. He wanted my cock and he was going to get it, especially because he was so willing.

But before we went on with this, there was something I needed to deal with.

"I think that first we should decide on a safeword," I proposed, and then he took the pacifier out of his mouth. When it wasn't there anymore, I was already a little sad about it.

Caleb was just so cute, especially with the binky in his mouth.

I was planning on making that something permanent between us. Whenever he was with me, he would always keep the pacifier between his lips, and it wasn't up for discussion.

"How about… *cockroach*?" He asked, rolling over on his back. I almost asked myself if he was also into pet play, but I didn't dare ask him that question. I just didn't think that it was appropriate for this moment.

"Cockroach?" I asked. I knew that it didn't matter which safeword he chose, as long as it was something he was okay with and that I wasn't going to get confused with, but I still wanted to know why he picked it, and I had no idea if he was going to answer my question or not.

He chuckled, rolling over on his back again. "Is that something I should answer?" He asked, rolling his body one more time. Every time he did that, he made my prick stir, and I was already thinking about how much I wanted to fuck him, making his ass feel so much pain that it would never be the same again.

"You decide, and especially if you want to be punished. You already know that I'm not the kind of guy that holds back," I warned, and he liked that. Caleb was loving everything that was happening between us, and that in turn was erasing the reservations I had about our little playdate.

He shoved the pacifier back into his mouth, rolling over on his back yet one more time. It wasn't that it was annoying, but that it always struck me a little odd. If Caleb wasn't into pet play, then he was surely doing everything to show me that it was something he could get into.

"I wanna be punished for being a naughty boy," he said, widening his smile. He smiled so beautifully and even though I knew that his teeth weren't professionally treated, they were still perfect.

Bright white, straight, not crooked at all – not even in the slightest. Meanwhile, I wasn't someone that bothered with going to the dentist often. It wasn't that my teeth weren't pretty, but that they could be better.

Regardless, I wasn't overly conscious about them or anything of the sort. It was just something I was pointing out to myself.

I picked him up again, taking him to the crib that was on the other side of the room. If the people here in Hope River found out about this room, they would bring out their pitchforks and other things that could hurt us.

They really were overly conservative, something that sometimes was an advantage, but other times, it was mostly annoying.

"I wonder what you're going to do to me," he teased even though the pacifier was still in his mouth. Seeing that, I just couldn't take it without doing something about it, which was for that reason I smacked his butt, hard.

And there was one more thing that was annoying me, and it was that he still had his shirt and pants on. I just couldn't have that, and I was going to do something about it.

I put him in the crib and then snuck my fingers under the band of his pants. He didn't do anything to stop me, and I watched his eyes carefully to find out if I was crossing a line or not. I was happy that it wasn't the case, and thus I finished lowering his pants.

When I could finally see his diaper, I could already feel the pre-come seeping out through the slit in my little cockhead.

This was only the beginning of our little playdate, and I was already in love with it. I could already imagine myself doing this many more times with him, and I was pretty sure he thought the same way.

His smile was still wide with the pacifier in his mouth, and he wasn't trying to hide it. Why should he? I asked myself, remembering that his teeth were godly perfect, and so were his lips.

They were so pinkish and kissable. I didn't know much about Caleb, but I could tell that he wasn't someone that kissed often, especially because of the city where we lived. Given that he was gay, he had to keep everything about that hidden.

I cupped his balls through his diaper, applying some pressure. It was enough to make him moan and close his eyes. When he reopened them, I could tell how much he loved this. He wanted more of the same and I was going to give him exactly that.

But then, I retreated my hand. There was no point in giving him everything he wanted at the exact time that he wanted it, I pointed out. If there was something I was good at, it was making littles like him beg to make their wishes real.

"That was a little anticlimactic," he pointed out, his voice sounding a little funny because he was speaking when the pacifier was still in his mouth. It was something I needed to remediate, and it was for that reason that I smacked his butt again. Given that he was padded, he didn't feel most of the strike, and thus I didn't have to worry if I hurt him or not.

I pointed my finger to his face, saying, "You are only allowed to say things when I want you to, okay?" And I wondered if he was going to take that well, and he did.

He didn't use his safeword or anything of the sort, which would have been disappointing, and especially so now when I was getting into the right mood. No longer was my mind worrying about the fact that some people could think that I was taking advantage of him.

He nodded. By this point, it was basically the only thing he could do.

I could see his diaper, but it wasn't enough. It was for that reason that I also took off his shirt, and now that it wasn't hiding his torso from me anymore, I held back a breath.

It wasn't the first time that I was seeing someone so pretty, but there was still something different about Caleb, and I couldn't put my finger on it.

And the fact that I couldn't do that was a little annoying, to say the least.

I put my hands under his armpits and then lifted him up like he weighed no more than a hundred pounds and really was a little boy. There was a bed on the other side of the room, where I sat with him. I spread him out on my lap and then lowered his diaper.

I noticed that it was already a little wet, and I didn't think that it was because of his pee or anything like that. It was thanks to how hard he was. Caleb was rock-hard and realizing that made me feel even stiffer than I already was.

"I don't have any mercy for you," I warned and I waited to see if he was going to use his safeword or not. When I realized that he wasn't, I smacked his buttcheeks. We hadn't decided on how many smacks I should give against his asscheeks, but it was okay. I was going to continue the punishment until he was shedding tears, and I didn't think it was going to take too long until that happened.

After all, I could already see that the sides of his eyes were getting watery.

CHAPTER 5

Caleb

I didn't think it was going to start with me spread out on his lap, but now that it was, my heart was beating like a jackhammer. I was biting pretty hard on my pacifier, feeling the first smack on my butt. It was harsh, but very much deserving. I was naughty and deserved to be punished.

I could feel my ass exposed to the air around me, and it was marvelous. Even though it was a little cold, I loved it. I could feel that Rhys thought the same way, which was the single reason why he was hard right now. I could feel his prick pressing against my butt, and it was sending shivers down my spine.

Even though I didn't see his hard cock yet, I knew that it was big. So big that it was imposing, menacing, and frightening. And yet, those things only made me want it even more than I already did.

It was for that reason that my mouth was salivating. I couldn't stop thinking about his hard cock going into my mouth, and I was hoping that it was something we were going to do soon.

"And there's much more where that came from," he promised and I knew he was telling the truth. The punishment rules were something that we would have to establish another time. Right now, we were focused on this punishment. I knew that I was going to get at least 20 smacks on my ass, which was something I was looking forward to.

When it came down to it, I loved being naughty and then punished. I knew that Rhys thought the same way, too.

I just nodded. There was no point in doing anything else, and he knew that.

It was for that reason that he lifted his hand over his head and then brought it down with force, smacking my ass one more time. It was absolutely marvelous, even though it was also just as painful.

I could feel the pain traveling to all points of my body, and I could do nothing about it. I felt my body jerking and yet it happened for only a second. The pain was everlasting, but I was getting used to it.

I was so hard as well. I knew that Rhys was aware of that, which was one reason why he was letting me rub my pee-pee against his thigh, which was thick and heavy, and also incredibly hairy. I loved it, and I wanted to be kissing it and roaming my hands around it, and I knew that Rhys wouldn't be opposed to that.

I felt his hand moving around my butt, almost as if he was caressing it and softening it, or almost like he was telling me that the pain was worth it. He didn't need to be doing that, for I already knew that it was very much worth it.

"Everything I'm doing is for your own good," he murmured, maybe even more to himself than to me. Sometimes, it was difficult to figure out what he was thinking, but maybe he was feeling a little sad that he had to punish me so early in our little play date. But he was just playing his role, especially when I was so naughty a couple of minutes ago.

I then felt one more smack against my butt, and my body jerked one more time. I could feel the tears coming out, but I was holding them back. If they were thinking that they were going to ruin this moment, then they were going to be disappointed, I thought, even though I knew that tears didn't feel anything.

And then, more smacks, and I already lost count of them. Counting them didn't matter right now, anyway. What mattered was enjoying this moment as much as I could, and even though my body was in pain and my ass was stinging, it was very much worth it.

When Rhys was finished, I was even smiling. Rhys chuckled, seeing that. He loved it when I smiled, and I loved his reaction as well.

It was one more thing showing that we could be right for each other, even though it would be limited to this space and kind of 'relationship.' I didn't think it would ever develop to anything more meaningful.

After all, I was only his little in this BDSM club and he was aware of that.

I felt his hand moving away from my body and then I fell onto the floor. Wrapping my arms around his legs, I felt how warm and thick they were, which was already soothing my heart. If there was one thing that Rhys was good at, it was comforting me, even after he punished me so hard. I put my head on his legs, closed my eyes, and then breathed loudly when I felt his hand on my forehead.

He was caressing it as he said, "It was for your own good, and I hope you can understand that."

I still had my pacifier in my mouth, and thus I knew that I couldn't say anything. The pacifier was basically for two reasons, and one was to keep my mouth shut, which was working right now.

And the second reason was to comfort me, which was also working. I couldn't be going through this moment without it.

Minutes later, when he pulled his hand back, he stood up slowly as he allowed me enough time to move away. I crawled away from him and then sat on the floor, noticing that he was making a beeline to the other side of the room. I wondered what he was going to do there when he showed me exactly what that was.

The room where we were was so big that it even had a fridge, a stove, and a small bottle in one of the cupboards. He filled it with milk, put a pot on the stove, turned on one of the flames, and then heated it with water until it was lukewarm.

I knew what he was going to do, and I was looking forward to it. So much so that my eyes were blinking. I couldn't hide the excitement on my face, and it was telling.

Rhys turned around, noticing it. He chuckled and then came over to me after turning off the flame of the stove. He was holding the baby bottle in his hand, and I already knew what he was going to do with it. He was going to put me on his lap again and then was going to feed the milk in my mouth, which was something I always dreamed would happen with me one day.

I was so excited that I was giddy, which was something that didn't happen often in my boring life. It was always so mundane, and it showed. Even something as basic as what we were doing was already making me so overly happy that I couldn't stop smiling.

There was a big, Daddy chair by one of the walls of the room, where he sat. He patted his thigh with his free hand, and then I went there, crawling.

I was always going to be crawling around in this room because I always fantasized that I was much younger than I really was. I still wore diapers, after all.

Even though, only in the club and never in my house. I just couldn't wear it there because I didn't want my parents to find out about it.

"Come here, little one. There's something really nice I'm going to do for you."

And it wasn't like I needed a second invitation. I just went there and Rhys was so strong that he picked me up with only one of his arms. It was definitely something that I didn't imagine happening, and I was happy for it. I felt his strong, powerful arm around me, and it made me feel safe. Feeling safe was definitely something that didn't happen often in my life. I wished it did.

I didn't say anything, remembering that the pacifier was still in my mouth. When Rhys wanted me to say anything, he would just take it out.

He rolled me over on his lap slightly and then nestled me in his right arm. I could feel his arm against the upper part of my back, and it was just as strong and muscular as before.

Noticing that I still had my pacifier in my mouth, he took it out gently and then placed it on the right arm of the chair. For the time being, it was going to be there, and safe and sound.

"Open your mouth wide, little one. I'm going to give you some of this delicious milk," he said and there was nothing else I could do other than to obey him.

And when the teat of the bottle was in my mouth, it was like stars were exploding in my mind. It was just so good, and I could imagine myself spending many more minutes doing this and nothing else.

CHAPTER 6

Caleb

Rhys even put his hand on my belly, caressing it while he still fed me the milk. It was formula, so it was a little more than milk. It was just as delicious, though. It was slightly warm, which made it perfect.

I didn't think I had drunk anything so good in a very long time, and never before did I feel so safe. Even though my parents liked me, they could never make me feel so safe.

He kept on brushing his fingers against my belly and time appeared to be moving in slow motion. Or maybe it was passing a little too quickly.

When I reopened my eyes, I just found out that the baby bottle was already half full, which was a little alarming.

If I drank too much of the formula, I would have to pee and mess my diaper, which was definitely something I was looking forward to. I did mess my diaper a couple of times before, when I was all alone in this BDSM club, but it was different then. It wasn't as fulfilling as it was now. It was like my body was melting.

I closed my eyes again and when I reopened them, I realized that Rhys was moving the bottle away from my mouth. I just checked it and I noticed that it was empty, which was something I was expecting, but it was still surprising. I was just surprised that it happened so quickly.

"Did you like it?" He asked, his finger brushing against my

belly button. The way he was doing that was so enticing and also a little erotic. I was hoping that our night was going to end with him inside of me, but I had no idea if he was even considering that. Some things about what he was thinking were easy to figure out, but others were quite difficult.

I nodded. I could speak now because I didn't have the pacifier in my mouth, but I had no idea if I wanted to. I was a little and quite young in terms of 'little age,' and thus I wanted to keep myself within the realms of the world I created for myself.

"Good. Now, I'm going to put you in your crib and then you can relax in it. When you're feeling better and want to do something else, just tell me."

He put his arms around me, picked me up, and then took me to the crib. I was already feeling a little sad that I wasn't going to be on his lap again, but it was understandable. It wasn't that I was feeling anything close to love when it came to Rhys, but it was almost like it was that.

When I was on the mattress in the crib, I lied down on it. Curling up, I closed my eyes and when I thought that something was missing, I realized that it was the pacifier. I was just going to stand up and ask for it when I noticed that it was already right in front of my face.

It was Rhys that was holding it, of course. It couldn't be anyone else, and I didn't expect any differently. When I tried to snatch it out of his hand, he pulled it away from me quickly, and it moved with the speed of a thunderbolt.

I was a little disappointed, and I even pouted, which was something that I actually did often. It was my way of showing that I was cuter than I really was. Not to mention that it always helped me with getting what I wanted.

"Did you think I was going to forget it, little one?" He said, and I knew that it wasn't a question. I didn't answer it, and Rhys wasn't disappointed.

Then, he moved his hand with the pacifier closer to my mouth and put the teat between my lips. I expected it, and thus I wasn't surprised when I felt it nestled between them, making me feel like a proper little one again.

The taste of the teat was still the same and just as good. It tasted of chocolate, which was definitely something that I didn't expect from this pacifier. There was no denying that this BDSM club was high-end, and that was reflected in the admission price.

It was a little pricey, but definitely worth it, especially when it meant that I was going to be with Rhys many more times in the future, hopefully.

I didn't say anything, but I definitely wished I was a little older in terms of ABDL age so that I could say 'thank you, Daddy' which would definitely melt his heart. I knew that Rhys liked that sort of thing.

I lied down on the mattress again, curling my body into a fetal position. If I didn't have the pacifier in my mouth, I would definitely be sucking my thumb. It was just as good and comforting, after all.

I closed my eyes and I didn't know if I was going to fall asleep or not. Chances were I could, but I still shouldn't. I was going to have classes tomorrow morning and I didn't want my parents to get worried about me. I told them I was going out to meet some friends and I was hoping that they were going to eat it up just like all the other times they did.

I heard Rhys walking away from the crib and then sitting on his rocking chair. He picked up a book and then started to flip the pages, reading them.

I didn't know what the book was about, but it appeared to be engrossing. I wanted to be on his lap again, but I knew that I couldn't be in two places at the same time.

Sucking on my pacifier, it was like time was moving so slow and I just couldn't hold back how much I wanted to sleep. And I did nod off, though not without feeling like I was missing something.

Maybe it was Mr. Bitsy, my teddy bear. He was a stuffed toy like all the others, but also different. He was special to me, and he was always going to be a 'he' to me. Whenever I thought of him, I always thought that he was more than a toy with some tears and holes.

Our relationship was a little weird, and it was definitely something that my parents thought they should change about me. It was for that reason I didn't talk to them about it, I remembered.

The room was warm, the mattress was comfortable, and even though I was naked, I knew that things were going to be fine. It didn't matter what was going to happen in my life. So long as I still had Rhys as my Daddy, he was going to keep me protected.

Or maybe I was just overthinking it. I didn't think that he looked at me as anything more than his little one that showed up in this BDSM club some nights.

I must've fallen asleep because when I woke up, I realized that a lot of time passed, and I noticed that thanks to the huge clock hanging on the wall, above Rhys' head. Thankfully, there was still more than enough time until I had to go back home, so I wasn't worried.

But when I was better aware of my surroundings, I felt my bladder full. It was like it was going to burst, and I needed to do something about it. The first thought that came into my mind was that I needed to find the bathroom as soon as possible, but then I realized that I was still in the same room and that I was also still wearing my diaper.

I wasn't supposed to go to any bathroom to do anything, I thought. I was supposed to pee in my diaper and mess it. When I was finished, it would be so messy that Rhys would have to change it, which was something I was looking forward to.

I sat on the mattress again, letting all the pee that was in my bladder out. I didn't say anything as I noticed that Rhys was slumped in his chair. I imagined that it was quite comfortable, though nothing beat sitting on his lap and nestling my head on his wide, firm chest. I just couldn't wait until I was doing that again.

Seconds later, when I could finally feel the smell of my pee in the air and the warmth in my diaper, Rhys opened his eyes. His stare snapped to me, and I knew that he had just one thing he could say to me.

He stood up slowly as he then said, "Looks like someone just messed his diaper, and that's unacceptable."

CHAPTER 7

Rhys

And I was going to do just that when I heard hurried footsteps approaching the door. For a moment, I thought little of it, but when they stopped suddenly and I heard someone rapping on the door, I knew that something was up.

My heart was already speeding up again, which was something I hated. I was in the mood to change Caleb's diaper, and now this was happening. I felt like destiny was playing against me.

Caleb took his pacifier out of his mouth, his eyes showing his seriousness. He was worried about what was happening, as he should be.

"Rhys, what's going on?" He asked, but then I waved my hand up and down to soothe his racing thoughts. He didn't need to be worried about anything because we weren't doing anything wrong, and I was going to deal with whatever was unraveling here, too.

He nodded once and slowly. I went to the door quickly, stopped behind it, and then peered through the small peephole.

I knew I was going to find someone behind the other side of the door, but I didn't think I was going to find an old man and also someone who appeared to be his wife, alongside the manager of the club.

They were a little impatient, and the old woman was even wringing her hands. She was so old that she could be my mother, and the man wasn't much better in that regard. They still wore clothes like they were going to be sleeping – or should be sleeping.

"Rhys, who's there?" Caleb asked and I turned my head around to answer him.

"It's an old man and his wife, probably, and also the manager. Don't worry. I'm going to open the door and then I'm going to ask them respectfully to leave us alone. If they don't, I'm never coming back."

"What do they look like? The old man and the woman, I mean," Caleb asked, his diaper looking fuller than normal. Noticing that, I just wanted to be doing something about it right at this moment. That little one shouldn't be in the crib without a new diaper, and thinking that was enough to piss me off.

I had no idea what the manager and that old couple were doing here, trying to get into the room, but I needed to do something about it as quickly as possible.

"I don't know how I can describe it. They just look old."

But I actually did know how to do that. A little, at least. The old man had short, pepper and salt hair. He was already going bald at the top, where the forehead met the hair.

His skin was slightly wrinkled, but it wasn't anything that stood out. I could tell that he applied anti-aging cream daily.

His eyes were jade-green and his nose slightly bigger than normal, like Caleb, which was something that I didn't like pointing out. There was a growing suspicion in me, and I wanted to brush it aside.

His facial structure was defined, a little square-ish and rough, but I could tell that it was much different when he was younger. He used to be handsome. There was also a sense of serenity in his eyes, which was something that I couldn't find often in people anymore.

He wore pajamas too, and they were light blue. They hugged loosely around his body and seemed pretty comfortable and light.

The sheen of sweat on his face told me that he came here in a hurry, and it was just like I pointed out before.

His body wasn't fat or too thin. He kept himself in shape, and there was no denying that.

The woman was noticeably shorter than him, hair short that fell in small waves around her hair. It was also going gray, but she dyed it often.

She tried to look like a ginger, but her black eyebrows didn't lie. She was a little uncomfortable with the color of her hair and felt even worse that age was catching up to her.

Wrinkles infested the side of her mouth. Her lips were thin, almost like they could disappear if she wasn't snarling at me right now as though she could see my eye through the peephole.

The marks of something on her face, slightly wet and whiteish, also told me that she was just getting ready to sleep before rushing over here. She was also with a sheen of sweat on her face and seemed more bothered by it. The thing that kept popping up in my mind was that she was hating how she was going to have to redo everything when she went back to bed.

Her nose, eyes, face, and pretty much everything else about her told me that she could be Caleb's mother, which was something that shook me to the core again. I didn't want to have to deal with her right now, especially because it meant that I would have to explain why he had a diaper on, and also why it was soiled with his piss.

Her pajamas were light pink and hugged her body tightly. She didn't buy it just to feel better when sleeping. She picked that size because it had the right dimensions for her, and also because she was the kind of person that liked looking her best despite the circumstances where she found herself in.

There was no denying that she was quite vain, and it wasn't something about her that she would ever admit, too.

"Does the woman have short hair? Is it dyed... in red?" He asked, gulping. I had no idea what he was thinking, but it was worrying me as well.

I nodded. "Yes, she has."

"Let me see who they are," Caleb proposed and I didn't like it. What if he found out that they really were his parents?

And if they were, it wasn't like I would be able to do anything about it. They'd call me a perv and then report me to the police. It wasn't something that I was looking forward to, saying the least.

"No, you stay there," I ordered and I thought he was going to obey me, but he didn't. Caleb just pushed past me, which was something I thought he never would do. He wasn't a little anymore, which was a little concerning and also disappointing.

He wasn't a little 24/7, and it was what I was looking for in terms of relationship, or at least what I would be looking for if I were open to one.

He went on his tiptoes to peer through the peephole. My heart was speeding up even more than it already was, and I wondered what he was going to say. When his eyes widened suddenly, I knew that my worst suspicions were becoming real.

Those were indeed his parents, and we were in deeper trouble than I thought.

"Oh, shit. It really is my parents, and I need to get dressed. They can't see me with the diaper on."

I heard someone rapping on the door again. "Rhys, I know you are in there. They are Caleb's parents and they want to see him. Open the door so that we can talk."

I was fumbling a little, but I still remembered that I needed to get a hold of the situation quickly.

I couldn't let it get out of control, especially because I didn't want Caleb to think that I wasn't reliable and strong, as he thought I was. When it came to being a daddy, those attributes were primordial.

"You didn't come here with a change of clothes, but that's okay. Just put your pants and shirt back on, toss the diaper into the genie, and then I'll open the door. Hopefully, they won't notice that something is amiss."

"Good idea," Caleb chirped, smiling even though this moment was quite complicated and there could be several ramifications. He took off his diaper and I tossed him his clothes. He picked them up mid-air and then shoved them back on.

In no time at all, he had already gotten dressed again, even though he didn't have anything for underwear, which was probably making him feel a little odd.

It wasn't like it was holding him back anyway, though.

When I looked over my shoulder to make sure that he was prepared for it, I noticed that he was smiling. Now that I was thinking about it, Caleb was prone to smiling all the time, which was one other thing that added to his happy and bubbly personality.

He was always so cute that I just wanted to pinch his cheeks, even though I couldn't do that right now.

I put my fingers around the doorknob and then opened it, breathing slowly and once to make sure that the manager and Caleb's parents didn't suspect that anything weirder than this being a BDSM club was going on.

Unfortunately, it still meant that they just found out he was gay, and there was nothing he could do about it. He was going to have to suck it up and if he needed further support, I was going to be there for him as well.

Nevertheless, I was worried about it. I was worried about Caleb.

CHAPTER 8

Caleb

"What the hell do you think you were doing there?" My father asked rudely, almost like he was going to jump out of the seat and rip open a hole in my neck. He was furious and I could tell that in the way his nostrils were flaring.

He still wore his pajamas, as did my mother. They were both concerned about me, even though it was also much more than that.

They were worried that I was truly gay and that nothing could be done about it. No therapy was going to convert me or could ever change me. I was at least happy that they didn't find out about the little side of me, which could have been catastrophic.

Had they found out about it, they would already be threatening me with not giving me their inheritance, which was something that frightened me.

I knew that studying in college wasn't going to help me get a job. When it came to the world of job applications and securing one, knowing the right people was primordial, and I just didn't have friends in high places.

"I was just having some fun, and I'm already an adult as well. I know that I don't live in my own house yet, but I'm planning to change that. When I can and when I have enough money for it, I'll be moving out of here and then I won't have to tell anyone about what I'm doing with my life, much less you."

I knew that I was also being rude, but there was no other way around it. My parents were the kind of people who respected firmness, being certain about one's own words, and I was showing that right now. I was doing this one thing that I didn't do often, which was looking directly at their eyes.

"As long as you are living under our roof, you have to tell us exactly what you're doing. And tonight, you lied to us.

You told us that you were going to see some friends, but after some digging, we found out that you were doing promiscuous things in that BDSM club. Just thinking about that hurts me."

"Well, then don't think about it. Don't think about me. Just forget me already and everything I do," I shouted, throwing open the door of the SUV and then jumping out. I stomped over to the house, slammed open the door – though without damaging it, thank goodness – and then opened the door of my bedroom with the same strength I used before.

I slammed it close, fell onto the bed, and then sighed. I felt like a huge weight was lifted off my shoulders, and I also felt much lighter because of that. I was relieved, in the end, that things happened this way.

Nevertheless, I was worried about something or, rather, someone. I was worried that Rhys was thinking that I wasn't worth the effort. It wasn't that we were dating or anything of the sort, but that I was already imagining that he thought I wasn't even worth doing some play dates with, and it *was* something I was looking forward to.

I didn't even know how my parents suddenly thought that they should snoop around what I was doing with my life. It wasn't like all the other times, when they thought I was with my friends. Either someone tipped them off, or I was a little careless this time when I lied to them.

To be honest, something about it was bothering me, other than those things, and it was the fact that I had to lie to them. I wasn't the kind of person that enjoyed lying and it showed. I just wasn't good at it, and what happened was pretty much the only lie that I was keeping alive.

Now… It didn't matter anymore, and there was only one other lie that was going to replace it, and it was that I was a little. They could never find out about that part of me, given the stigma around it.

I reopened my eyes, finding the ceiling fan above my head. I was just looking at it, almost admiring it. I was thinking about so many things, and none of them made any sense. What made sense was reaching out to Rhys, but I didn't think he would even bother answering me. Even though I knew he was a good guy, he didn't want to be associated with me anymore.

After all, there was the whole thing about him being much older than me, and also when my mother shouted, multiple times, right to his face, that he was a perv.

I shook my head, finding it a little bothersome that the ceiling fan wasn't spinning. *I need to do something about that*, I thought, jumping off the bed and then going over to the little switch device on the wall.

I flipped one switch up and then the ceiling fan started to spin, even though its speed wasn't enough. I felt like I needed to be hearing the sound of the fan spinning, and I wasn't having that right now.

It was as though the littlest of things could infuriate me now. I never even thought about the speed of the fan before, and now it was getting on my nerves.

Thinking that, I pressed another button, and then the ceiling fan started to spin a lot faster, drowning out the sound of the front door opening slowly. That was my parents, entering the house.

I had no idea if they were going to come up to my room, but I was hoping they weren't. I was hoping that they were going to leave me alone, even though that was unlikely to happen.

I just fell onto the bed again, glancing up and then jerking when something in my pocket buzzed. It had to be my phone, and thus I wasn't surprised when I picked it up and found something different and enticing. It was the same guy that I was with at the BDSM club, and he just sent me a message.

Rhys: Hey, little one, is everything okay? I know that you went through a lot today, and I want to make up for it. I want to say that I'm sorry for dragging you into it, and it shouldn't have happened.

My heart hurt. I didn't think he was going to say he was sorry about it. After all, he was a biker and I always assumed he was irreparably cruel and unwilling to say that he did something wrong. It wasn't that I thought he did something wrong, though, but that his apology came as a surprise.

Caleb: I should be the one saying I'm sorry. After all, my mother shouted to your face that you are a perv, and I know that it isn't like that. They just can't accept that I'm an adult now and they want to be controlling me all the time, which just can't happen anymore.

There was a moment of nothingness and I wondered if he was going to reply back to me. He might have sent me that message because he just wanted to get that out of his system, which was understandable. I didn't think that he even cared much about me, but I was hoping that wasn't the case.

Rhys: I'm not going to hold it against her, if that's what you're worried about. I understand where she's coming from, and it didn't hurt me. I've heard worse.

Caleb: I'm much more relieved after you said that. Unfortunately, I don't think I can ever go back to that BDSM club. Not right now, anyway. Or not anytime soon, and I know it's disappointing, but there's nothing I can do about it. We need to at least wait until the dust settles.

Rhys: I know you are worried about it, but there's something we can do, in case you want to have more play dates with me. I thoroughly enjoyed the one we had, and I especially enjoyed punishing you.

My heart was thumping in my chest like a speeding horse. I didn't think he was just going to propose that. I thought we were always going to be meeting up at that BDSM club, but that was before shit hit the fan.

And maybe there was something we could do.

CHAPTER 9

Caleb

My hand was itching to do it. I was naked, in the bathroom, but my mind kept going back to what Rhys said. Our little promise, and it was so dirty that it couldn't be shared with anyone.

Not even my friends... But it wasn't like they mattered much anyway. I didn't have many, and the ones I had didn't come here looking to hang out with me. They didn't know anything about what I was doing, and I wanted things to stay that way.

Right now, I just wanted to jerk off so badly, and my cock was hard and begging for me to do that. It had already been weeks, and it was really asking of everything I had in me.

All of my discipline, how much I could control myself, and even I was surprised by how much self-control I had. Or at least, by how much of it I was displaying.

Some nights, when nobody was looking and I knew that everyone was sleeping, I did some pretty naughty things. Nothing that involved jerking off, though, since that would be breaking our rule, but it was something close to it.

It was dark outside and also incredibly quiet. I could even hear my own breathing. I was sweating a little, but it was okay.

I was just trying not to think about Rhys and his perfect, delicious body. He had rippling muscles and I could just imagine myself gliding my hand over them, feeling every curve and pretty much every part of him.

I knew he wanted to do it, but since my parents were keeping a close eye on me this time, I couldn't. I was trying to behave, even though it was difficult.

It was like I was trying to fight against my own nature, which was something that actually happened pretty often in my life. I was always trying to be someone I wasn't.

I heard my phone buzzing. It was on top of the sink and, glancing at the screen, I just found out that it was a message from Rhys. It couldn't be from anyone different, I thought amusingly. I even felt a smile creeping across my face, and I wanted to hide it.

It wasn't like Rhys could activate my camera and see me through it, but I still felt like his eyes were on me. I felt as though I was being examined and monitored all the time, which was something I found out I wanted after discovering that I was a little.

Rhys was a biker and a very controlling one. He was always checking up on me.

I took another breath, picking up the phone. I was already feeling a little better with it in my hand, but it wasn't enough.

If Rhys even had the slightest suspicion that I was about to break the rule where I wasn't supposed to touch myself, we would have to meet up. Then, when we did that, he would have to put a diaper cage on me. It was slightly padded in case I had to pee while it was on, and just thinking about that was making me want to do it.

The problem was that Rhys would never do that unless he thought it was necessary. He wanted to find out if I had enough self-control. I was showing him that I had, and it was working.

I read his message with his voice, which was something I always did.

Rhys: Hey, little one. It's dark, I miss having you in my arms, and I just want to say how much you mean to me. You are the most important person in the world to me, which is why I want to make sure you are following our rules. Even though you can lie, I advise you not to. If you do, I'll find out and you won't like what other punishments I have in store in case that happens.

My breathing quickened. I craved his punishments, but I also knew how painful they could be. It was fine though, anyway. I was getting used to them, just like I was getting used to this part where I couldn't masturbate and had to cut off that pleasing, rewarding part of my life.

Typing on the screen of the phone, I shot back a message.

Caleb: It's fine, really. I'm on my bed, lying on it, and thinking about you, although not at all sexually. I'm thinking that I'm in your arms, that I can feel the warmth and reassurance that only you can provide me, and I really love you.

The last part was a lie, but it was a lie that he agreed on. He always said that he wasn't ready for another relationship, and I could see where he came from with that. I also didn't believe in love, especially because I wanted to be focusing on other parts of my life, even though what we were doing was almost like we were in love.

I took another deep breath in, letting the phone fall back down on top of the sink. I didn't need it right now, and I knew that it was going to take Rhys a lot of time until he texted me back.

My hands circled over my belly, looking for my cock. It was hard, and I could almost feel that my come was going to shoot out through the slit. I sure as hell hoped that wasn't going to happen, especially because Rhys promised that we were going to meet up again and that it would happen at an unspecified date.

He said that it was going to be a surprise and that he would catch me off guard when he announced it. It was for that reason that I couldn't jerk off right now – not to the point of cumming, anyway. If I came and then I went to our full, unhinged date and didn't have much cum in my balls, he would know the truth.

And yet, I suddenly found my hand around my prick. I was almost hoping that he was going to text me again, just so that I was taken out of my reverie.

I could picture Rhys lifting up his shirt, showing me his rippling and flexing muscles, sweat drops streaming down his skin.

My mouth was already watering, just thinking about it. The man was always so perfect it was like he could never be anything different.

And then, the phone buzzed again, almost catching me off guard. For a moment, I was so lost I didn't even know what to do. But then I stopped fumbling and glanced at my phone. The screen was black, but I was sure that it was Daddy that just sent me a message.

Daddy... Thinking of him that way was already making me feel more excited than normal. I could imagine myself falling in love with him, even though it might never happen. Our lives were wholly different, after all.

I had to pick up the phone regardless of what I was doing, though. When it came to Rhys, he was more impatient than I thought a person like him was. If I didn't answer his message right away, he would surely punish me.

We would have to meet up after that night when everything went wrong in the BDSM club and then he would lock a chastity cage on me, claiming that I couldn't control myself, which was pretty much the truth.

And yet, I didn't want the chastity cage. It would make it so Rhys could even control when and where I could masturbate, and that wasn't something I was looking forward to. He would have even more control over me than he already did.

And even though it was exciting to be under his control all the time, sometimes it was a little too taxing. Just like right now, when I wanted to jack off until I was orgasming. He always asked me to be patient because he was going to take care of that soon, I remembered.

The screen turned on and I could read his message.

Rhys: Turn on the camera and be quick about it. I want to see you. I want to see the real you and how much you want me. You have about a couple of seconds until I realize that something wrong is going on and that I need to intervene.

Oh shit, that message was sent only seconds ago, which meant that I didn't have much more time. He wanted to see me lying on my bed and nothing else would do. It was for that reason I was already hurrying up while putting my clothes back on, even though it was dangerous and I almost lost my balance and fell over.

Even my parents, who were unfortunately still home, were probably wondering what it was that I was doing. They could come up here, corner me, shoot me several piercing questions, and I would stumble with my words, looking helpless.

A moment later, when I flopped onto the bed and turned on the screen of the phone again, Rhys just texted me again.

Rhys: Well, since you didn't turn on the camera in time, we're going to need to do that thing we agreed on. We are going to have to meet up in person and then you will be rewarded with a chastity cage. And don't even try to hide from your duty. You know it won't work.

Even though his demand was scary, I had a smile on my face. I was finally going to see Rhys again in person, and it was going to be thrilling. The only problem was that I was going to have to sneak out of the house to do that, though.

But I could do it. No matter what happened, I was going to do it.

CHAPTER 10

Rhys

I pulled over far away from his house. I knew that my Memory could make a lot of noise, to the point of waking up an entire neighborhood, and so I had to be careful. It was dark and the night was beautiful. It was serene, inviting me to do a plethora of things, like going out with my mates on a hunt or just fucking around until there was nothing left to do.

I shook my head, stretching out my neck. His house could be seen in the distance and all the lights were turned off. I wondered if he was going to manage to sneak out of his house without my help. If he needed it, I was here to provide it to him.

Time was passing and I was getting a little impatient. If it took Caleb too much time to sneak out of his house, I'd have to intervene. I knew that meant possibly running across his parents, but that was okay.

Even though I didn't want to admit it, I was beginning to feel something strong for him. Perhaps it was the fact that I could finally play around with a little one that was making me feel that way about him, but I... didn't know for sure.

The neighborhood where he lived was nice. Big, ample houses that looked too similar, trees that were frequently pruned and taken care of, grass that was often mowed with a lawnmower, and most of the properties even had swimming pools and dedicated areas for barbecue.

Those things, coupled with the fact that all the houses were built far away from each other, made this place quiet and peaceful. In fact, all the noise I was hearing was from the nearest freeway, and that was a little scary.

I just didn't want any residents finding out that a biker was here at night. Not only would there be a lot of gossip flying around the next day, someone who wasn't in their right state of mind could even call the police on me, and that was definitely something I couldn't let happen.

I was drumming my fingers on the console of the bike when I noticed a shadowy figure emerging from the back window of his house, relieving me. It was Caleb and he was jumping out of his house, which brought a smile to my face.

I stopped drumming my fingers on the console of the bike and perked up. He fell to his knees when he landed on his house's lawn, but then stood up right away. He didn't hurt himself, which was relieving. I thought he did, in which case I would have gone there to make sure he was okay.

He turned around, finding me. Even though I was so far away I could barely make out his face, I could tell he was smiling. Caleb probably didn't go to the dentist as often as he should, but he still had such perfect teeth that they always made me want to see them.

I felt like it was taking forever for him to come where I was, or maybe I was just imagining it. In what could be less than a minute, he was right by my side, and then he swung his leg over the seat of the motorcycle, sitting down on it.

He wrapped his arms around me and I could see ourselves doing this many more times in the future. He with his arms wrapped around me, his body against mine, and I suddenly found myself wondering what it would be like to have a boyfriend.

"I missed you so much," he said and I perked up again. I didn't think he would ever say something like that, especially right after wrapping his arms around me and inching his head so close to my shoulder that I could almost feel his breathing.

I didn't say anything, hoping that he wasn't thinking he was going to become my boyfriend. I just wasn't… Ready for a new relationship, and this was nothing more than us having some fun that we otherwise couldn't have in this town, right?

I was hoping that was the case, but there was no point in making it a bigger issue. Caleb was with me and, apparently, he even managed to sneak out of his house unnoticed. None of the lights were immediately turned on, which was relieving.

That meant I could leave the neighborhood without having to create a lot of noise. With that in mind, I turned my head so that I could glance at Caleb over my shoulder.

"Ready to go?" I asked and he nodded, smiling with closed lips. I felt like kissing him right now, which was something I thought I would never say.

I was still trying to keep our arrangement as professional as possible, but as time passed, doing that was becoming increasingly difficult.

He tightened his arms around me, and then I turned the bike and we took off, though slowly. I wasn't making a lot of noise with Memory, but I was still worried.

I was worried that someone was going to wake up, peer through the window of their bedroom, and then spot us riding down the road in front of their house.

Minutes later, when we were finally out of the neighborhood, I let out a breath of relief. I was safely out of it and proceeding to where my house was. It didn't look anything like the one where Caleb lived, but that was okay. I was pretty sure he wasn't going to mind it.

When we got there, he lifted his head off my shoulder, checking out my house. His eyes moved up and down, and left and right, processing all the details of it like his life depended on it.

"I never thought you lived in a place like this one," he whispered and I had no idea how to take that. Was he surprised or disappointed by what he was seeing? I didn't know, but I didn't ask him about it anyway.

I pulled over in the driveway, lifted the garage door, and then pushed Memory until we were safely inside it. Then, I closed the door of the garage and we stepped inside the house itself. I turned on the lights and Caleb went into the living room, turning around slowly as he checked out everything his eyes could see. It was like he was taking mental notes of everything that was around him, and it was then I noticed that he was quite perceptive, especially when something piqued his burning curiosity.

"It really looks like a biker's house," he murmured and I also had no idea how to take that. I never thought he would say something like that, but it didn't matter anyway.

I knew that my living room had been better, especially when I first moved in here. A layer of dust covered the floor and the furniture, the couches had some holes and tears, the TV's right side was broken and the screen was slightly shattered there, and the light hanging from the ceiling wasn't as bright as it used to be.

Regardless, Caleb didn't come here to scrutinize my house. He came here for me, and we were finally going to have the fun we had always been looking for. It was only our second play date, but I had so many things planned for him, and I was certain he wanted to do all of them.

I turned around slowly and then he was right by my side, his hand grabbing mine. "Come with me to my bedroom. There's something I need to find out, and I want to know if you behaved these couple of days without seeing me. If you didn't, you know your punishment will be hard and long-lasting."

And I didn't have to worry if I was crossing a line or not. Caleb had his safeword – Cockroach – and he could use it anytime he wanted.

CHAPTER 11

Caleb

I was on his lap, biting my bottom lip. Even though he couldn't see my eyes, I knew he was assessing what I told him. I told Rhys that I behaved during the time that he wasn't with me, and I had no idea if he was believing me or not.

I could feel his hot breath against my neck. He was naked, but not entirely so. He still had his pair of briefs on, and it was dark, contrasting perfectly with his white skin. The hair of his legs brushed against the skin of my legs, shooting waves of pleasure through my body.

The warmth of his body pulsed out of it, enveloping me. His fingers brushed against the back of my hand, and it was almost like time was moving in slow motion.

His room was dark, but enough moonlight still snuck through the windows and the blinds. My eyes could just about make out the shape of his legs and that he was much taller than me, to the point of making it so my feet couldn't reach his.

In fact, being on his lap was reminding me of how much smaller than him I was. Rhys was also not holding anything back. His cock was hard and it was pressing against my butt, making me wonder what it would be like when he was inside of me.

Our night had just started, but I was pretty sure that it was going to be a long one. I was still going to be home before my parents noticed I was away, but that was okay. I wasn't worried about what they would think of me in case shit hit the fan again.

"So, this whole time you didn't even touch yourself?" He probed, his fingers brushing against the nape of my neck and then his nose breathing a cloud of breath on my skin, making it tingle.

"Of course not, Daddy. I've been waiting for you and for this moment this whole time. I would never disobey any of your rules," I responded and my voice was low and throaty.

It couldn't be any different, especially when his fingers were gliding up my arm, feeling all the little hairs that I had there.

Even though it was dark, I could see his fingers and hands finishing that movement, and it was thrilling. I could feel my heart thumping and my body sweating profusely.

"Well, it's time to find out if you are telling me the truth or not," he said, sneaking his fingers under my pair of briefs and then enveloping them around my pee-pee. It was small in comparison to his, but it was okay. It was supposed to be that way, especially because it made me feel much more like a little, and that was a plus.

He began to stroke my pee-pee, forcing me to shut my eyes and then tilt my head back until it was resting on his other shoulder. His chest was pressed against my back, and his nipples brushed against the skin there, sending ripples of pleasure in my body.

His nipples were hard and like big, heavy pebbles. I wanted to be sucking on them, but without his okay and without him proposing it, I wasn't even going to bring it up.

My pee-pee was hard immediately, which was the reaction he was hoping he was going to get from me. I could feel his hot breath against my neck again, and I knew he was satisfied.

"Okay, so it looks like you really behaved these last weeks. But that doesn't mean you've been a good boy, and we need to do something about that."

And the longer this was going on, the more I was beginning to think that I could see myself as his boyfriend. It would be difficult and I would have to deal with my parents, but it could also be one of the most rewarding things in my life.

And something I thought would never happen already was. I

was considering it. After our little playdate was over, I would have to tell him what my real feelings for him were.

Still moving his hand up and down along my prick, he murmured into my ear, "Wanna find out how long you can last?"

I nodded. There was nothing else I could do, and I knew that was the truth. His prick was just so hard, and I just wanted this to go to the next level so that I could wrap my fingers around his manhood and then give him the handjob of his life, and also the most breathtaking blowjob. And perhaps even something more rewarding than that.

"Good. There's so much more I want to do with you, and we should start by doing that," he promised, increasing the speed with which he was giving me the handjob.

I could feel his hand shooting up and down on my little pee-pee, and it was getting so hot around me that I was sweating much more than before. I could feel my breathing quickening, almost like I was running out of oxygen.

Even though he was seeing the reaction I was displaying, he was only increasing the pace of his hand. His hard, gargantuan rod was still pressing against my asscheeks, and I knew that he was planning on penetrating me, and perhaps that was going to happen tonight.

And then, when I felt that my climax was about to wash over me, he stopped. His hand stopped moving up and down on my dick, and I was left wondering what happened.

When I finally regained consciousness of my surroundings, I turned my head around slowly to meet his eyes. He was staring back at me, but his eyes were full of love and lust - and also even sinfulness, which was something I always knew he had, but it was still frightening, especially seeing it in person like this.

I didn't have my pacifier in my mouth, in which case I wouldn't be able to speak like I was. I also didn't have my diaper on. This just started and we didn't have time to do that yet. When we did, I knew that it would change this fundamentally.

"Why did you stop, Daddy?" I asked, my voice even throatier than before. He was ruthless when he did that. I knew about orgasm denial, but I never thought that it was in his plans.

I knew that I was supposed to be punished, especially because, before now, I said some awful things, but I still never thought that orgasm denial was one of his punishments. I didn't think it was fair, but I wasn't going to use my safeword, regardless.

"You don't deserve to come, not right now, anyway," he said and then smiled devilishly. I knew he was going to say something like that, it was still a little frightening and definitely infuriating. And yet, I wasn't going to say that to his face, especially because I didn't want to piss him off even more than he was.

I just lowered my head, showing him my disappointment. He didn't like it, pushing me off his lap so that I was on his bed, and then he stood up slowly and went over to his closet. He opened it, picking up something plastic, but that definitely looked durable. The chastity cage.

"It's pretty small and I know you can use it daily. I know you are a virgin and that this is especially hard on you, but things will be so much better when you learn everything it has to teach you."

I widened my eyes immediately. I didn't think he was going to propose that right now, even though it was enticing. I could just imagine myself wearing the diaper cage, walking around in it, going to college with it on, and all the while remembering that I couldn't touch myself because it was in the way. It was going to be painful, but certainly rewarding.

"Daddy, but I don't know if I can," I said and he just smiled. Of course he was going to smile. Rhys knew that I was lying when I said that I didn't want the padded chastity cage. Even though it was small, thin, and light, someone could notice it and would probably start asking questions about it.

"You can, and it's for your own good. You're going to feel so much better when you have the chastity cage on you," he said, coming over to me, and then I turned around and went on all fours on the bed, making it easier for him to secure the chastity cage on me.

And he did, locking it with a key and then tossing it into the right-side pocket of his pants. Even though I made a mental note of that, I knew it wasn't going to amount to anything.

He patted me on the back and then said, "See? This is so much better. You can stay with me for a little while longer and then we could finally do that one thing you've always wanted."

I knew what Rhys was talking about, and my heart was thus thumping in my chest.

CHAPTER 12

I supposed there was no denying it. That strong, impactful feeling that I had in me was love, and it couldn't be denied anymore. Not to mention that Caleb was now becoming even more like the little I had always hoped he was, and he was better for it.

I could even see that it was making his mental health better. He was smiling more often and was getting more used to sneaking out of his home when we needed to meet up.

He was in the backseat of the bike, his arms wrapped around me. I could feel his chastity cage pressing against the lower part of my back, reminding me that, tonight, I was going to take it off him. He was going to be smiling from ear to ear when he realized that his punishment was finally over and that I could take his virginity.

Even I was excited for that, as I should be. My heart was thumping in my chest.

I parked Memory in the garage, closed the door, and then went inside the house with my little one in tow. He was following me by taking short steps, like a toddler learning how to walk. His hand was so small, especially in comparison to mine, I thought now that my hand was grabbing his.

"It's time to take off your cage," I announced and his eyes shone brightly, making me feel like pinching his cheeks, which I did.

I went to the bedroom with him, made him sit on my bed, and then I pulled out the small key that was in the pocket of my pants. I showed it to him, and his smile widened.

He was so happy that he was almost jumping even though he was seated on my bed. If he started doing something like that, he would have to be punished, which was the single reason why he was behaving.

It took weeks of him living with the padded chastity cage that looked like a diaper, but he was finally a much more malleable boy, and I loved that about him. So much so that I was also jubilant that I was finally taking off his cage.

When it was unlocked and then I slid it off him and I could see his prick, I was already thinking about giving him the pleasure that he came here for. I could see it in the way that his legs were shaking, and he would be even happier if made him come.

And it was at that moment I made a decision, and I was going to stick to it.

"I love you," I said, catching him off guard. I knew that he was going to be surprised by it, but the look of shock on his face was still telling of what he was feeling. Caleb thought the same way, and he wasn't hiding it.

A tear came out and rolled down his cheek. I couldn't just watch it without doing anything about it, and thus I swept my finger on his cheek, getting rid of the tear. He didn't even flinch. Caleb fully trusted me and he was a much better person thanks to that.

I could see his eyes trembling slightly, and I was feeling a little sorry for him and also for the beginning of our supposed relationship. It didn't even start properly and it was already dying.

A moment of nothingness and I wondered what he was going to say. If Caleb didn't say anything and just stormed out of the house, I would be fine with that. After all, he was still around college age, was most likely thinking about his professional career, and not much more than that.

I was probably overwhelming him and I felt like a jerk for that.

I stood up slowly, crossing my arms over my chest and then shaking my head in disappointment.

"I'm so sorry I said that. I didn't mean to. I was just getting carried away."

I closed my eyes and thought he really was going to leave the house, but then I felt his hand settling on my shoulder. It caught me off guard, and I whirled around immediately. I found his eyes, and they weren't just trembling anymore. He was shedding tears and it was unexpected.

"I love you too, Daddy," he cooed and I knew that it meant much more than that. "I was the same. I wasn't thinking about falling in love, but it happened. I'm in love with you as well, and I think about you all the time.

I think about living the rest of my life with you as your little one, and I know you want the same. That's why we need to leave Hope River as soon as we can."

I felt his fingers digging into the skin of my shoulder slightly, and then I couldn't help but wrap him in my arms, lifting him up. The smile that wasn't on his face before showed up suddenly, and I could tell how jubilant he was.

It was certainly warming my heart.

I put him back down on the floor gently, wiping my eyes with my hands quickly. I shouldn't be crying and I wasn't. I was only getting a little more emotional than I usually did, which was certainly something that didn't happen often in my life, especially as a biker. I'd gone through so much worse before and now this was having this heavy impact on me.

"Well, I guess there's no point in wasting any more time," I said, reaching out with my hand and picking up his pacifier. He was already opening his mouth, waiting for me to put the pacifier between his lips.

And I did that, loving the way that his lips wrapped around the teat. And then, he was suckling on it like he had nothing that could ever bother him.

Our life together was going to be riddled with me punishing him, but this time, it was going to be different. It was going to be about my love for him, and it couldn't be any different.

"Are you going to put the diaper on me, Daddy?" He asked and it was much more than a question. He was pleading for me to do that, and I was more than willing to make his wish a reality. I didn't even think about how I was going to do it, even though I should be.

After all, it was the first time, in a very long time, that I was going to put a diaper on someone, and I barely knew how to go about it.

I picked up the diaper, tore open the package, and then collected all the skin creams, talcum, and pretty much everything else that he was going to need so that he smelled perfect. The smell was going to be lingering in the air and I was going to be thinking about it, remembering it for hours on end even after it faded away.

"Of course, little one. I'm going to put a diaper on you for the first time and it's going to be different. It's not going to be like the chastity cage, which I know you loved."

He was smiling and I didn't say anything about the fact that he talked while the pacifier was still in his mouth. It was its purpose, after all. It was supposed to keep his lips shut. Maybe I was going to do something about that, but not right now.

I spread out the diaper on the mattress after taking off his pants and the rest of his clothes. He shifted over so that he was with his butt resting on the diaper. Then, after wiping his sensitive regions with a handful of wipes, I smeared the region with all the skin creams that I'd picked up before, and then tossed over some talcum for good measure.

When I was done with that, his smile was even wider, even though the pacifier was still between his lips.

I sat on the bed and then lied down on it, putting the little one between my arms, and then I brought him close to me so that his head was resting on my chest.

Brushing my fingers over his forehead, I murmured into his ear, "I love you so much I'm already thinking about leaving this town tomorrow. Wanna come?"

He craned his head so that his eyes found mine and I knew his answer before he said it.

"With you, I think I can go anywhere."

CALEB'S EPILOGUE

"**M**om and dad, you can't change my mind about it. After all, I'm an adult now and I can make decisions for myself. I know it's hard for you, but it's how it's supposed to be. I'm supposed to be independent now, and this guy here really is the man I want to live the rest of my life with."

My mom's hands were hugging each other right in front of her chest. Dad's body showed that he was more relaxed about it, but he was still tense. When I said that I was moving out with Rhys, he was shocked.

He never thought that I was going to propose something like that, or rather that I was going to make such a decision.

Mom took a deep breath, stepping closer to me. I knew what she was going to do before she did it.

She grabbed my hand, caressing it. "Caleb, is there really nothing we can say to change your mind?" She asked and I already knew what to say. Even though it was going to hurt her heart more than it already was, it needed to be said. It needed to be brought out so that she understood I wasn't kidding about it. I was being serious.

"It's my decision, mom. I'm going to be moving out right now and even though I don't ask for your approval or support, it would be great if I could have them."

She took a deep breath, clearly showing that, if she could, she would be changing my mind about it right at this moment. Even though she didn't like that I was gay, she was coming to terms with it, and it was working. She just never thought that everything was going to have to be happening so quickly and suddenly.

After all, one moment I was with Rhys, who was also by my side right now, and the next I was telling them that I was going to leave for New York City, where I was going to build my life with him.

She eventually let go of my hand, and I was happy she did that. Her trembling hand was making me feel much more nervous than I already was.

And I wasn't going to lie about this: even though I was certain of my decision, it still came with a heavy price. So much so that I could almost feel it weighing down on my shoulders.

Noticing that I was feeling lonely, Rhys grabbed my hand. It was big and comforting like always, and I didn't expect any different. I knew that it was always going to be the way it was.

I turned my head to meet his eyes and I did. His hand was enough, but finding comfort in his eyes was even better. They were so warm even though their color suggested otherwise.

"I'm here for you, no matter what happens." That's what he said and I knew he was telling me the truth. It was exactly the only thing that was populating his mind right now.

My father took a step toward me and I thought he was going to dis me for the decision I made, but then he said something different. "I'm so sorry I treated you harshly before when I found out about the fact that you are... gay." And even though he had to say it, the word still hurt him.

That was okay, though. He was going through a lot, and I knew that he was going to get used to it. I wasn't straight. I wasn't going to give him grandchildren.

He retreated his hand, which was also trembling slightly.

"It's okay. You can visit me in New York City whenever you want."

I felt Rhys' hand tighten around mine, and it told me that he wasn't convinced by that. He was probably thinking that someone so homophobic should never get near us again, but I wasn't that heartless. Actually, people always said that I had a heart of gold, and it showed.

I could never even consider punishing anyone for anything, and my father was certainly not an exception.

"We are going to do that."

It was the only thing he could say at the moment, and it was much more than I expected.

"Well, good luck going to New York City," my mom continued and then we bid farewell and they went back inside their home. My former home. I wasn't going to be coming back here in a while, and even after I decided to visit them, I wouldn't be excited about it.

Even though it could probably make me feel nostalgic about our former life together, it wasn't going to erase all the bad memories I had of the place. Every damn time that my parents were putting me down, making me feel forced to have a girlfriend, thinking that something was wrong with me, and all those other nightmares.

I was just content that they were starting to lament what they did, and maybe from now on we could start things over.

And yet, I wasn't thinking about that right now. I was thinking about my Daddy, who was also my boyfriend, and also much more than that.

I threw my arms around his neck and he pulled me up, his arms going around my back. When our lips connected, it was like fireworks were exploding in my mind.

"There are so many things I want to do with you when we are in New York City."

"On our first day there, we should visit the Statue of Liberty. My friends have always talked about it so much and always said so many good things about it that I'm impatient to go there."

"Really?" He widened the right side of his lips slightly and abruptly, and I could feel his musk and the smell of his perfume. They were so perfect, intoxicating my lungs. "All right, then. I don't see any problems with doing that."

RHYS' EPILOGUE

Even though I thought that it was going to happen differently, I knew that my little one was ready for it. Before going to New York City, we were spending a night in the motorcycle club and most of the members were out, probably riding across the town, drinking, killing time, maybe even raiding some houses. Those were just things that they did as their lifestyle and I wasn't going to judge them.

I reached out with my hand, putting my fingers around the little loop and then plucking the buttplug out of his ass. There was a squeaking sound and then a pop, and I could see that the buttplug did what it was supposed to do.

His orifice was slightly wider and looking more adequate for when I penetrated him, which was what I was going to do soon.

He had his pacifier in his mouth and was sucking on it gently. He wasn't supposed to say anything or even scream or do anything that would make too much noise. It was a rule we agreed on, and the only thing that could even come out of his mouth was his safeword.

If everything went according to plan, he wasn't even going to need it.

The bottle of lube was on top of the nightstand. I picked it up, screwed open the cap, and then poured some of the liquid into my hand. It was slightly cool, thanks to the liquid itself, its nature, and the dropping temperatures outside.

Going to New York City while it was snowing was going to be a memory that would forever be in our minds, and I was already even more excited about it than I was before.

I could feel his body trembling slightly. Little Caleb was somewhat worried that I was too big, and he had every reason to be concerned about that.

I slid my hand over his legs, feeling them. His skin was unbelievably soft, and just the way I liked it.

Then, spreading some of the lube in his orifice, I felt the inside of his rectum, and it was warm and slightly tight. We also got tested for STDs and we knew we were both clean.

There was no point in worrying about any of that right now, and I wouldn't be doing this with a condom, anyway. It was just not at all satisfying, losing one's virginity while a piece of rubber was in the way. It happened to me before and I wouldn't recommend it.

"I'm going to be careful with you, and you don't need to worry about it," I announced, grabbing his legs and then playing with his little orifice a couple more times. Caleb moaned, his fingers grabbing the bedsheets and then digging in them. I wasn't even doing anything that could make him feel pain, but it was like he was feeling that.

I stopped, making sure that he was okay. His breathing was slightly ragged, but it looked like he was doing all right.

"And I'm going to do the things you've always been waiting for," I said after playing with his asshole for a little while longer, feeling its texture, its shape, loving it, and then even rubbing my finger inside it a couple more times. Each moan that escaped his mouth was like music to my ears.

I dragged him to me, prodding his orifice with my prick. He felt it and then shut his eyes, almost permanently.

I applied a bit more force using my hips, though without thrusting with them, and then I broke through the initial barrier. I was inside my little one, and it was warm and still a little tight. I kept on easing myself further inside of him, and then it wasn't too long until he was moaning and groaning softly, his hands suggesting that he wanted me to keep on going.

"Are you okay?" I asked and he nodded. I was happy that I got the confirmation I was looking for. He was deep enough for me.

The delight on his face was almost something I could touch with my hands. It was, I would certainly be all over it.

And when I reached the end of his tunnel, scraping his prostate, I started to roll my hips. I was doing it slowly, making sure that my pace wasn't hurting him more than it already was.

Even though I did everything possible to loosen it up, I was just too big for his butthole. I was so massive that I probably needed one extra boyfriend, even though I didn't think it was something that would ever happen. When it came down to it, little Caleb could get dangerously jealous of me.

I picked up the pace moments later and then I came in him. I could feel my milk filling his rectum and coating his walls, and I moaned and groaned, only pulling out of him when I knew it was over.

And when it was, I noticed his orifice trying to close itself in, but it wasn't working. After getting ravaged by my rod, he was changed for the rest of his life. His orifice was much wider now, which meant that penetrating him was going to be much easier next time. And yes, that meant this was going to happen plenty more times in the future.

I fell onto the bed with him in my arms, and then we fell asleep. The coming morning was going to be full, but we were both prepared for it.

The End

Looking for the other books in the series?

1. Firefighter's Punished Little
2. Cop's Punished Little

And check the next page and read a sneak peek for book 1. Leave your **review** for this story. Your feedback helps me improve!

TEASER: FIREFIGHTER'S PUNISHED LITTLE

ABDL MM Romance (Small Town Littles – 1)

Blake

When it came to diapers, nothing could hold me back. That was why I dissected that one diaper behind the glass panel, wishing that I was loving it with my hands. But I couldn't and the reason for that was pretty simple. Every time that I diverted my eyes down, I caught sight of the price tag, realizing that it was too high, especially for someone living in the middle of nowhere.

A small town. Hope River was the kind of place where people over 60 came to retire and I just couldn't imagine myself living here for much longer. For one, finding gay dates was pretty much impossible, not to mention the nasty repercussions that would come. People would shun me, think that I was less than human, and I didn't want that ruining my life right now more than it already was.

I wasn't going to say that I was poor to the point of not having food on the table, but it wasn't good, either. I had food. I could go to the local farmers' street market and buy whatever I wanted, but it wasn't enough. I wanted more than that. The food commercials that popped up on the news that I couldn't get my curious hands on? They allured me all the time to a life I knew I would never have.

On a side note – and a very important one at that – I couldn't show my true self to others. I was a little and always had been one. I refused to grow up and get older. People looked at me and thought that I was still underage, even though I just crossed that infamous adult-enough-to-drink line and could drink pretty much anything, not that it mattered, anyway. I didn't want to spend my nights drinking my sorrows away. That wasn't how I saw the world and I'd rather kill myself before letting something like that happen. It just would never.

The diaper that was in the store was unlike anything I'd seen in my life and it would fit me. It wasn't a diaper for babies or little boys. Rather, it was something built differently. A small town meant that most people that lived here were pretty old and Hope River wasn't any different.

I couldn't stop wanting the diaper that was in the store and I wanted to rip it out of it right away. My hands were pressing against the panel and I could feel as if I was melting into the store, ready to become one with it. But it was pretty difficult convincing myself that I could spend 5000,00 dollars on that one single diaper, especially given that it couldn't be used more than a couple of times.

That's right. The diaper was built so differently that you could wash and dry it and it would still be usable.

Not to mention the special material that it was made of, that it was supposed to be extra comfy, how it let the skin breathe, that it was supposed to make you feel like you were walking in the clouds, and all those things...

Alek

"I'm so sorry about this. I was just going there and I didn't see you until it was too late," I said, feeling very awkward about it even though I knew it was something I could fix, especially with a nice dinner made by me. I was pretty sure that the guy I was helping to get up was one of the many in town that thought I couldn't be a cook, even though I was. A long time ago, when I didn't even live in this town, I used to be a cook. I used to cook pretty much everything and anything I wanted, which was one reason why I enjoyed life so much. I wasn't going to say that it was bad, but it used to be better, though.

His eyes were shocked by what I was doing, which was nothing short of expected. After all, I wasn't just helping him up by holding him with my hand. I actually looped my arm around his torso, feeling how much smaller than me he was, not that it was something I always paid attention to whenever I was helping someone. This time, it was just something I noticed, which was weird. It was the first time I noticed that about someone.

I didn't know this guy's age, but he appeared to be young, maybe even underage. His cheeks were buttery-smooth and even though I couldn't touch them right now, I was pretty sure they were also cotton-soft. But just like it was with everyone else in this town, I shouldn't even be harboring those thoughts about him. He was probably straight and was with one of the girls that lived here.

I looked for a ring on his finger and I couldn't find any. That didn't mean he wasn't taken, but I wasn't going to give myself false hope. I kept that in mind as I pulled him up, still finding it a little funny the way he was looking at me. It was as though he was nothing more than a lost little rabbit in the woods that spotted a wolf for the first time. He was disoriented, confused, and wanted to ask me several questions.

I wasn't going to lie and say that I didn't want to stay here to answer all the questions he had for me, but I didn't have enough time for that. So much so that I had to wave my hand over my head and say, "Don't worry about me. I'm going to be with you guys soon. There's just this tiny little mistake I made and that I'm going to fix."

They were my friends, the firefighters. They were rushing over to the building where violent flames were gobbling it up. I could even see the smoke billowing up from where I was. I had no idea if the guy I helped up was aware of it, but it was possible that he wasn't. After all, he appeared to be lost in his own thoughts.

"No, it's uhh... okay. You didn't see me," he said when he realized I wasn't supporting him anymore. Not only was he very small and short, but he was also feather light. I didn't enjoy boasting about it, but I was pretty sure that I could pick him up with just one arm, which wasn't something I did every day...

OTHER MM ABDL BOOKS

SERIES - SWEET PACIS

Bikers! This series is filled with them. Sweet littles that fall in love too easily, dominant and possessive bikers, and a lot more. It's perfect for binge-reading.

1. My Caring Biker
2. My Loving Biker
3. My Protective Biker
4. My Obsessive Biker
5. My Possessive Biker

SERIES - REGRESSED

Littles, obsessive Daddies, and lots and lots of age play. This series is as steamy as it's heartwarming.

1. Gifting Crayons
2. Sugar Mister
3. Loving Little Chris
4. Bedtime for Cody
5. Little Crayons

ABOUT THE AUTHOR

Jerry Hastings biggest love? Writing MM ABDL books. He can't go a day without imagining worlds where littles find their Daddies and live their HEAs. His stories are peppered with diapers, pacis, and a plethora of coloring books.

His best-sellers are 'Quarterback's Little' and 'My Caring Biker', which are books that he'll always remember fondly. Check them out on his author page.